M. J. Wilcoxson

The Vestal

A Collection of Articles in Prose and Poetry

M. J. Wilcoxson

The Vestal
A Collection of Articles in Prose and Poetry

ISBN/EAN: 9783337371876

Printed in Europe, USA, Canada, Australia, Japan

Cover: Foto ©Andreas Hilbeck / pixelio.de

More available books at **www.hansebooks.com**

The Vestal:

A COLLECTION OF ARTICLES IN PROSE AND POETRY, COMPRISING
A SHORT ESSAY ON

Origin and Destiny,

Given through the Mediumship of

MRS. M. J. WILCOXSON.

———

live in hearts we leave behind is not to die."—*Thomas Campbell.*
"What I had I gave.   Forget the poet, but his warning heed.
And shame his poor word with your nobler deed."—*J. G. Whittier.*

———

CHICAGO:
RELIGIO-PHILOSOPHICAL PUBLISHING HOUSE,
S. S. JONES, PROPRIETOR.
1872.

INTRODUCTION.

Having been many times solicited to publish some of the poems which have been given to me, I made the experiment by sending out those little waifs, "The Midnight Prayer" and "The Festival Night," and such has been the demand, especially for the former, that I am encouraged to reprint it, in connection with other poetic productions, some of which were first given impromptu at the close of my lectures. Suffice it to say there was a time in which these impromptu poems were frequent, and of so marked a character as bearing upon subjects suggested by the audience after my taking the stand and passing into the inspirational or entranced condition, that they have proven good tests in the minds of many of my hearers. Though not knowing, or having the faintest idea of what subject might be presented, a sort of previous mental illumination would take possession of me, in which detached, broken clauses and stanzas would sweep across my mind, with no consecutive connection, but, on the other hand, fragmentary and fractional; and, to my surprise, I found that when more perfectly under control in my public labor, these parts of stanzas, at first seemingly disjointed and unsatisfactory, were so arranged and filled out as to produce a perfect

poem.   Being urged to reproduce these effusions,
I began the experiment alone in my room by call-
ing upon the same intelligences, invoking the presence of these controlling teachers; and though
there may not always be a complete duplicate, I
feel that there has been little difference in language, and that the original sentiment or moral
has been strictly preserved.

I am satisfied that with proper cultivation of
mediumistic gifts, great benefit may be secured
thereby.   Important questions, bearing upon the
welfare of both the medium and the community,
may be answered by our translated counselors, in
a manner to avert all uncertainty, and I hail the
day in. ' *the good time coming*" when mediumship will stand among "the lively oracles," and
be protected as it deserves.   Now, of all things
included in the grand school of Human Progress,
mediumship, the principle by which the translated reveal themselves, is the least cultivated, the
most abused, and the most difficult to preserve in
its purity, of any power which has at last come to
be recognized in this nineteenth century.   Once
admitted to the magnetic realm, in which the finest susceptibilities are made to assert themselves,
it is impossible for the subject to conform as before
to established usages.

A new life is awakened.   A true medium is
always behind the scenes.   He becomes a non-
conformist, simply because a magnetic quicken-
ing is to him what young spring is to old, snow-
crowned and frosted winter.   He is let loose; he

must grow. He is taken out of old, conservative, ice-bound regions, and put directly under a magnetic sky. Suns and showers become plenteous. His old nature is thawing out. He has been run in a mould; and now he melts beneath the sunbeams of a new life, and commences running outside of moulds! Propriety-loving conservatism says it is disastrous, fatal! But his new sun, his new sky, his new stars, and all that is NEW, as reflecting the spontaniety of Nature, who never wore a chain, have stamped a new name and a new life upon his being, and he reflects precisely the truth in himself and all things coincident to him! He can no longer *lie*, and that is why he is so strange! Whatever his nature is, he acts it. Whatever the nature of others, he reflects it. Nor is it really optional with him what fraction of the universe, either physical or mental, he shall reflect. He is simply a mirror, and the truthfulness and value thereof depend upon circumstances. And there is often such a *refractive*, as well as *reflective* quality in the mirror, that even good observers and honest investigators, from ignorance of the law, lose the revelation.

When the possession of mediumship is regarded as the link connecting two worlds, and is as well preserved as the cable which connects two continents—when one-half the care and pecuniary outlay is expended thereon which every grand enterprise demands before it reaches perfection, we shall see less failure, and come into possession of one of the greatest of all levers in raising the hu-

man race to a true manhood. No matter what it
may cost us in the way of experiment, no matter
how much of dross may wrap the atoms of fine
gold in curtained embrace, the gold is still there,
and capable of being separated from all the worthless surroundings, and its value is an established
truth which can not be denied.

What we need most of all now is, that having
the truths of inspiration established, we study how
to secure the highest perfection and prevent the
counterfeit circulation from supplanting all confidence in the genuine. I know that every earnest
and true medium has been compelled to carry a
load never lifted by any other soul, and simply
because it was *his* burden. It was his or her honest trial of strength and duty which no other soul
could carry. It was "his day of judgment," in
which individual merit must be tested, and for
itself alone. A few, at least, "chosen" from the
"many called" have, with blistered feet and up-
lifted eyes, walked the fiery furnace of ordeal with
no vanity of thought, but with the hope of perfection burned into the deepest grooves of the
soul! Oh, who will write their tears, their suppli-
cation, their touching entreaty, their humiliation
and sorrow for weakness and mistake, as breathed
in the ears of angels and recorded on the pages of
truth! How harsh and unrelenting the world of
mortal judgment, as it passes criticism upon the
failures of mediums! But compared with the tri-
umphs of ocean steam-navigation to-day, what a
stupendous blunder and failure was that little

experiment of Robert Fulton's, when at a com-
paratively snail-like pace he mapped the distance
in his tiny steamer! And compared with the net-
work of lightning-wires which now encircle all civ-
ilized realms nearly, how meaningless and silly
the school-boy kite of a Franklin with its simple
glow-worm light, its fire-fly sparks of revelation!
And still farther, compared with the length and
breadth, the power and importance of this West-
ern Republic in a sanitary and commercial point
of view, as now related to the great centers of
trade and government in the old world, how small
the promises of a Columbus—how rash and profit-
less the enterprise he engaged in! But while
"man proposes" "God (or eternal truth) dis-
poses," and "from the acorn grows the towering
oak," but not more surely than from the hum-
blest and the meanest of all discoveries bursts
forth the grandest and the most sublime of all
revelations! Surely it is not a small thing which
our dear departed, and the spirits of "the just
made perfect" have done, in arousing our latent
reason, and awakening our spiritual nature; and
though the same sunshine which warms into life
our choicest plants, gives life to the gross weeds
of our soul-garden also, let us be vigilant, and
bravely work on till we find them eradicated.
The harvest shall in time reward our labors.

Without regard to distinction of creed or party,
but with the spirit of fraternal love and confidence
in the better instincts of the soul, I dedicate this

little work to my co-laborers in the field of human reform, and cheerfully grant to all dissenters from our faith the right to criticise and decide, each for himself, and not for another, the claims herein presented.   Sincerely,

M. J. WILCOXSON.

THE VESTAL.

Origin and Destiny.

Probably no subject has in modern times excited more inquiry than *the origin of the human soul*, and with all the evidences which go to support "the development theory" on the physical plane, it will be seen that the real problem of *origin*, as regards the soul itself, is left in obscurity. The assumption of the Materialists that soul, or spirit, is the result of a certain structural perfection, would entirely disprove immortality, for there could be in that case no guarantee of future life; the soul, or intelligent part, being purely the production of organic conditions. Destroy the conditions, then, and there is an end to all identity, and that which was dearest to us of all things in existence is rudely torn from us and forever annihilated!

If we follow the "development" theory, it does no more than trace the links of origin on the physical or fleshly plane. It can no better account for the first incipient evidences of sentient life than the old Materialistic assertion. It, in fact, traces the evidences of origin no farther than the rudiments of physical science, and fails to prove the doctrine of a future life. For if the *origin* of the human soul is to be found in the chemical cohesion of certain particles of matter, which evolve in that combination the principle of life, and a certain order or refinement of intelligence, it is self-evident that with the disorganization and destruction of the body that soul ceases to exist. Thus, while matter, in its essential atoms or particles, is known to be perfectly indestructible by all the tests of chemical science, the soul itself, which is capable of analyzing and subordinating matter in all the experiments and productions of the laboratory; this truly sublime Thought, which evolves science in itself. which confronts and subdues the wildness and stubbornness of uncultivated nature; the master-power which tunnels the mountains and bridges the chasms; which turns to account both fire and flood, launching out upon the once unknown ocean its princely palaces of art, and throwing across the storm-wrapped waters its cable of lightning, annihilating both time and space in the velocity of transmission—this grandest of all powers, proving identity of character and variety of talent, this, to which matter is the raw material, the mere clothing, is treated as *less than matter*, over which it asserts its superiority from the cradle to the grave!

If matter, then, be indestructible, it must be eternal, though it be so inferior to the intelligent Soul-Power which makes use of it. If eternal, it must be self-existent, for that which is eternal could not have been created. It had no beginning, and therefore, except in the organic or structural, it

has no ending.   As it thus becomes the clothing
of intelligent Thought, this Thought, or Soul,
which appropriates and subordinates, must be
the positive and superior power; while matter becomes to it negative, subjective and receptive.

Thus, that supreme Life-Principle which speaks
to us as God or Soul, is found robed in all the
changing patterns and garbs of Nature, while it
comes to us in multiplied, countless sentient be-
ings, of whom MAN is the highest mundane perfection.

All this host of intelligent creatures has been
supposed to have a creation, a beginning, and
"one fate alike befalleth both man and beast,"
said an ancient philosopher, who had no true con-
ception of the Immortal Principle.   And while we
can prove beyond dispute the eternity of matter,
many doubt concerning a future and continuous
self-hood of the human soul.   That which has
come to us, spoken to us, loved us, lavished upon
us the sweetest of sympathies and affections, that
which has been to us more than sun, and moon,
and stars; more than all the regal magnificence of
earthly nobility; more than all the jewels of court
and crown; more than our food and raiment, our
name and our only life—that which has been to us
the bright gateway of the soul itself; which has
kindled a new fire upon our home-altars; brought
down the glory of the firmament and enshrined it
in every beautiful form of art; that which has
called forth our love, our emulation, our human-
ity; which has taught us and trusted us, followed

us and saved us; that kindred soul-principle which has been woven into our very life, which has asserted its divinity, verified itself to our partial understanding and our love—surely that majestic and sublime REALITY must be as immortal as the crude material of which it fashions its decaying temples or weaves its fleshly vestment!

Then, where did the soul exist previous to its incarnation in matter? Where shall we find this mysterious presence, and what were its antecedent conditions? If immortal, how? For if not as self-existent and uncreated as matter, we can not prove its immortality.

Our conclusions are predicated not only upon philosophy but upon facts. It is a fact that chemical science has unveiled a world of causes and effects before unknown. It is a fact that simple intuition has mapped out the locality of an unknown continent, as in the case of Columbus. It is a fact that men are subject to sight, and sense, and hearing, which comes not within the domain of the physical; as in the case of Swedenborg, who saw at the exact time, the details of a fire hundreds of miles distant, and entirely beyond the scope of the physical senses. Hundreds of cases might be cited to prove beyond dispute the existence of senses superior to the physical plane. These senses take hold upon a new empire—are not limited as are the purely material senses, but sweep on from the plane of effect to the realm of cause. Chemistry can not explain the mystery, though it can resolve all kinds and proportions of matter from the solid or fluid state to the high-est degrees and attenuations of refinement; thus changing the qualities and properties thereof throughout the whole scale, till it reaches the sub-tle realm of spirit, able to grasp it still, and prove its indestructibility. But beyond that it can not go. The soul itself must possess senses of supe-rior potency to those which are dependent upon merely material conditions.

With the awakening of the soul-perceptions, which carry us beyond the limitations of finite and fallible sense into the empire of cause, we may find an answer to the most difficult problems which have hitherto baffled inquiry, because we dealt with them from the material standpoint. If it be true that we possess any one sense like clair-voyance, or intuition, by which we take cogni-zance of things or truths not perceived by the physical senses, the principle is established that there is within the soul such powers, and reason tells us that any power or principle subordinating even in degree the world of effects, must be meas-ureably superior thereto. The truly illuminated or inspired soul must possess such advantages of clear perception as that *the world of cause* may be as truly cognized as *the world of effect;* and seeing that eternal harmony must exist between cause and effect, the soul, by virtue of its own in-trinsic attributes, must eventually be able to ex-plain itself. This it partially does in the pro-phetic state. unveiling the events of the future, and it is not to be doubted that with cultivation, or even the liberation of the mind from enslaving dogmas, the intuitive or prophetic power would become one of the grandest of all aids in exploring the hitherto untrodden realm of soul science.

If, under any excitation or activity of the mental powers, future events may be portrayed, surely it must be as natural and legitimate a function of the illuminated thought to take cognizance of past events; and by what law is this accomplished but that of soul-perception? The soul evidently acts from the superior or objective plane, while matter is acted upon. As matter is self-existent, why is not soul likewise? As matter is the clothing in which soul arrays itself, it is evident they are co-existent. The soul-world may be regarded as the empire from which all force proceeds; and as the conditions of external life become responsive to the laws of the Superior, matter becomes the language by which soul becomes individualized, and identity commences. As matter elementally is known by its particled or atomic state, so soul is first known by its existence as a simple entity, and certainly not less immortal than matter, if as indestructible.

To the illuminated perceptions of the spiritual man the spaces of the superior or inner realm from which every order of life proceeds to individualize and ultimate itself is a vast ocean of the most sublimated and etherealized elements, in which float as a part thereof (the same as drops are a part of the earthly oceans and seas) these countless germs or soul-entities; all of which pre-

serve the spheric or globular form, and can not
be seen in any other character previous to their
inception in an individualized state. When this
commences, the duality of Being which is always
illustrated by the circle or sphere, being an in-
nerent principle, is outwrought by Nature's uner-
ring law, in the production of an organism which
shall be the sure exponent of that special order or
variety of life. In this process Nature always pre-
serves both the male and female principle, which
is fundamental to organization and propagation.
Thus, the soul-entity, or immortal principle, act-
ing upon matter, secures itself a structure by the
disposition of all the necessary parts, in which a
perfect machine, a most complete mechanism, may
connect it with the world of individualized life.
Here we find the primal law or principle (as regards form) the cellular and spheric, is repeated
throughout the entire structure, the solid parts
retaining the cellular, the fluid parts retaining the
spheric or globular. To use the words of another
writer, "Man is the microcosm, in which the mac-
rocosm, or greater universe, is illustrated," for
the reason that his structure is of a higher order,
and his mind capable of grappling with every
question and elucidating scientifically every law
of the universe, granting him full empire for his
scientific powers. And now we discover the perfect harmony of Being in the complete adaptation
and equilibrium of the two worlds to each other.
Here the soul-entity asserts beyond dispute its
own specific gravity or self-hood, which, as pro-

ducing character and determining destiny, belongs
to no other individual in God's universe. Having
accomplished this, sooner or later, by casualty,
disease or age, this now individualized soul passes
on to higher courts, throwing off the gross garb of
mortality, now laid aside as a rusty, worthless
vestment, but retaining the fine silken tissues
which have been woven into a spiritual body,
within the material laboratory. How beautiful
now its career, how grand its flight, if knowing
itself, and ripened by a cultivated and unfolded
intellect, it breaks from its chrysalis of mortality
and speeds on to its glorious home, and enters the
society of that "innumerable company," those
great minds over whom superstition and death can
have no power! Now buoyant with the inspira-
tions of a higher state it can gaze backward upon
the rough and stony road of human experience
with a philosophy and conviction it never knew
before. It sees how in its grosser, worm-like
state, the mechanism of that fleeting structure
was ever in motion, ever with ceaseless throbbings
and pulsations weaving out the shining web of
destiny with which the golden shuttle of immortality beautifies and completes the glorious pat-
tern of existence.

Day and night, the seen and the unseen, are but
the links in one mighty chain of Reality; and to
press on, with new empires, new Edens before us,
becomes an inspiring thought which robs our
fleeting night of its pain and darkness, and studs
our firmament with the fadeless fires of immortality.

ANGEL VISITANTS.

[Written for the Twenty-fourth Anniversary of Modern Spiritualism.]

O, I hear, I hear the patter,
  As of childish hands and feet—
On the table, on the carpet,
  On my head, my hands, my seat.
Drops seem falling o'er my person,
  All as if some joyous sprite
Would arrest my solemn thinking—
  And I feel a strange delight!

What is this? A tiny rapping—
  Rapping out the tune she loved!
Aye, the tune we sang together,
  When we last in wildwood roved!
Hear, O hear it! And she told me
  She would give it as a test,
Could she come and tell me truly
  Of her home among the blest!

Listen! listen! O, what music!
  Coming from the organ-keys—
Now it rises, now 'tis floating,
  Like a harp upon the breeze.
All around the room 'tis sweeping.
  How it thrills my feeble soul;
Now it seems to grow more distant,
  Upward now it seems to roll!

What is that! A pencil writing—
  Hear it glide along the slate!
What delicious spell doth hold me,
  As expectant thus I wait!
See, O see! it is a message,
  Written out before my eyes!
'Tis my precious child—my angel,
  Come to give me glad surprise!

2

Listen ! listen !   Do I hear her ?
   O, it *is* my darling's voice !
Ah, this is more than I could hope for.
   Shout ! let all the world rejoice !
Death is conquered—now victorious,
   O'er the grave the millions rise,
Pressing on to fairer kingdoms,
   Fairer empires, fairer skies.

O, what burden now so heavy
   I shall ever more despair ?
O, what trial now so fiery
   I shall cease the victor's prayer ?
O, what scoffing now can move me,
   O, what torture make betray,
As love's golden chain grows tighter,
   Gilding all my future way ?

Let us cease our childish wailings,
   Wandering amid our tombs ;
Light fresh fires upon our altars,
   Consecrate our mortal homes.
Let our lives be pure and worthy,
   Free from bigotry and guile,
Then our angel friends returning
   Oftener will upon us smile.

And when called beyond the river,
   We shall bravely mount the arch,
Where our tried and true companions
   In their love-lives daily march ;
And with those who went before us,
   We will sing the living word,
Which in blessing God's dear children,
   Shall by untold hosts be heard.

Then, O, shout the great salvation,
   Simple rap and murmuring bell ;
Shout the coming in of heaven,
   Shout the going out of hell !
Shout the death of fraud and error,
   Shout the life of every truth ;
Shout the final resurrection
   Of the soul to endless youth !

ODE ON WAR.

War, war, war !
When will his merciless tramp be stilled !
When will his roar be hushed !
What mountains of manly forms lie chilled,
 Their bones by his engines crushed !
When will his scorpion thrusts be stayed,
 And stayed all the hellish arts
By which his victims are constantly flayed
 At this bloody feast of hearts !

War, war, war !
I am gazing into your valley of bones,
 Created a smiling vale.
Around it I see all your costly thrones,
 Where you drove on the lovely, the sick and the hale,
Through fire and blood to your altar of lust,
Where you made the beautiful lick the dust,
And famishing millions without a pang
You smote with the stroke of your cruel fang !

War, war, war !
I am gazing—gazing into your past ;
 The valley, the valley I see !
I am counting the miles that measure the mount
In that valley of bones, and the peaks I count,
Where your victims, chained for these countless years,
Have paid you tribute of blood and tears,
Till creation groans with the ghastly pyre,
And the heavens are livid with blood and fire !

War, war, war !
Thou blasphemous braggart of earthly kings !
 Thou knave, and coward, and fool !
With thy empty titles, thy diamond rings,
 And sceptre of stolen rule !
How long hast thou taken that name in vain—
The GOD, who hath clothed both valley and plain
In robes of bloom and harvests of grain ;
And given in plentiful store each year
To toiler and tender a bountiful share !

War, war, war !
No more may the stolen, the purchased and sold
Be driven like sheep to your treacherous fold ;
No more by the lash of your impious power
Consent to be slaves, or honor your hour,
In this rush for gold—this lust for a throne,
Where unnumbered lives are the cost of each stone !
Thou hast left thy venom on fairest bowers,
Thou hast trampled our beautiful buds and flowers !
Thou hast all these gardens of heavenly fruit
Turned to a lair for both serpent and brute !
Thou hast held in thy craftiness shuttle and loom,
Scarce finding on earth for thy artifice room ;
And thus upon ocean, the air and the skies,
Thou hast laid thy full tribute, and robed in disguise
Of cant and pretension, thy infamous might,
By prating of JUSTICE and promising RIGHT.

War, war, war !
On the mystical waves of the future I see
When your empire of Moloch shall cease to be.
Through the curdled clouds and the blackened skies
I see the fair kingdom of MERCY arise.
Her ruler, long promised and long sought of men,
Shall lead the torn nations in UNION again.
Through the clashing of sabres and beating of drums
The sweet strains of Peace to my grieved spirit comes !
To the mangled and maimed, from the glory-wrapt sky,
The angels of God with sweet messages fly !
And I try to forget it, or bear the deep groan,
And the wearying sob of my suffering own !
Ah, *my own ! my own !* For their pains are mine !
In this terrible vintage I drink the wine,
And my heart is torn by this long delay—
This seeing my noblest the monster's prey !

War, war, war !
Tell me no more of thy conquering crown,
And thy royal rule, while thy victims drown ;
Tell me no more of thy roll of FAME—
I spurn all thy record of sin and shame !
Tell me no more of thy millions freed,
While chained they all are by thy tyrant-creed !
Tell me no more thy shallow excuse

For this shedding of blood—a ruse, a ruse !
But, beautiful vision, come nearer still ;
Flutter thy pennons o'er valley and hill ;
Bathe in thy radiant glory of LOVE ;
Over the EAGLE hold highest thy DOVE !
Oh, in life's Calvary, comfort each heart,
Bleeding and gasping 'neath war's flashing dart ;
Over the battle-ground, over the sea,
Waft thy still breathings, bid Tyranny flee.

Come nearer, come nearer—oh, in the death-hour
Tenderly touch them and charm with thy power.
Softly and sweetly, like dews of the night,
Put all these cravings for empire to flight.
Shatter the golden god's glittering car,
And lead on to conquest by Mercy's sweet star.
Beautiful vision, oh, hasten along
Breathe your glad tidings to earth's weary throng.
Mould with thy magic the heart of the king,
Over all rulers thy mystic spell fling ;
Roll in thy music, till, on its rich notes,
The banner of Peace in proud victory floats !

Then, war, war, war !
What shall be left thee but infamous name,
Echoed by valley, and cloudlet, and stream ?
While the souls whom thy engines of tyranny braved,
Shall find on the record their loyalty graved !
And thou with thy dotage, thy rattle of bones,
May grope 'neath the ruins of empires and thrones,
While the Judge of the heavens shall doom thee to night,
And bring in his rescued to Freedom and Right !

THE MIDNIGHT PRAYER.

[NOTE.—I will simply state, for the instruction of my readers, that an intelligence purporting to be Edgar A. Poe, has a number of times controlled my organism, both in the trance and impressional state. I am always in a lucid or clairvoyant condition while under such control, and see, or seem to see clearly, the pith of the poem. I am as a spectator, or unseen participator in the reality which is vividly laid out before me.

In this superior state, I saw Poe, desponding, and nervously excited, hurriedly start from his boarding-house, with a haggard look and apparent misanthropy, and rapidly walk in the direction of a bar-room. A beautiful boy of about eight or ten years, to whom he was devotedly attached in his sober moments, followed upon his track. Without speaking to the child, but seeming anxious to escape him, he rushed on, and soon the potent draught was doing its work of discipline. The faithful boy, with tender, sad solicitude, kept just in the back-ground, following the aimless footsteps of the unfortunate poet through all their meanderings, from point to point, till darkness crept down upon the city, and the busy throng of human life began to retire to their homes.

Lost alike to the love and hate of mortals, the poor inebriate sought with failing footsteps a lone path, which led up a hill-side in the suburbs of the metropolis, and at last sunk upon the ground. The wearied but devoted child still pursued the wanderer, and as soon as unconsciousness wrapped with its mantle the stricken man, he noiselessly crept to his side and laid himself on love's sweet, sacred altar, beneath the smiling stars of midnight. There, with his fair and tearful face pressed to the burning cheek of the wanderer, his dimpled hands clasped around the neck of the poet, both slept. At last the throes of returning consciousness and reason in the man, rolled off the sleeping sentinel, whose saving, trusting child-love is here set to the music of angels, and sends its burning appeal up to the high altar of every true soul.]

Once, in my madness, when mortals deserted me,
   Once, in delirium, all prone on the pave,
Once when the Furies seduced, and then thwarted me,
   In wild laughter shrieking beside my lone grave ;
Once, when conceited souls scornfully jostled me,
   Sped their fire-arrows of fury and hate,
Once, when to hell they condemned and then hustled me,

They, my betrayers, appointing my fate ;
When the night-curtains all lovingly shielded me,
And the Star-Angels let down their sweet light,
When the deep silence crept up and enfolded me,
And mother Nature wept tears at the sight ;
That once, when I thought that only God pitied me,
And all had forsaken and left me to die,
In the black darkness of passion that crowded me,
Something aroused me, with deep sobbing sigh !

Then, in the darkness I looked for intruder,
Wondered if any dear Savior was near,
Thought of meek woman as once I had viewed her,
Thought of my mother, though absent, so dear ;
Longing for rescue, and cursing my destiny,
Cursing the shams of a Judas-like age,
Cursing the sins of professional piety,
Dealing the hemlock to poet and sage.
Moments were ages, eternities burdened me,
Life with its pages confounded and frightened me ;
Life was a riddle, and I was expounder,
Never a problem unsolved or profounder,
Than in this crucible chased and confronted me,
Just as I lay on the Lethean shore—
Thus did my reason from prison just loosened,
Like a free bird scan the great evermore.

But, as my reason returned, some intruder
Kept breaking the stillness with deep sobbing sigh ;
And it strung my lone harp which the Ghouls had beat rudely,
With the mystical loves of the angels on high ;
Just then a sweet breath like the odors of Aiden,
Far sweeter than fragrance of Orient gale,
Fell full on my forehead, like vow of a maiden,
Or love of a mother, which never doth fail.
And then a bright meteor arched with its silver light
The dewy wet couch where still passive I lay,
Revealing a watcher who into the midnight,
Had clung to "poor Edgar" when men turned away.
There, chiseled in sorrowing, but radiant feature,
His damp locks all curling around his fair brow,
Lay Willie, companion, and watcher, and preacher—
And night was the altar, and speechless the vow !

Methought that in heaven his spirit was pleading—
　So calm and so still lay that cherub-like form,
And that he had breathed his last life-breath upon me,
　And leaped to the land where there's never a storm !
Methought that last heart-sob had broken the heart-strings
　And let the poor dovelet return to the skies ;
And I fancied I saw how it beat with its freed wings
　The measureless space of its own native skies.
And I fancied I heard how his holy petition
　Went up to my Father that I might return—
And then all the archways of heaven, in vision,
　Were lit by the love-lamps that ceaselessly burn.
And loud alleluiahs, all answering his pleadings,
　Swept down the broad spaces, and filled the grand aisles,
And soothed with their baptism my lone heart and bleeding,
　And struck low the Tempter, and scattered his wiles !

O childhood, I bless thee ! wherever thou strayest,
　Thou dost gather the buds of affection most rare—
Not in pitiless tones or cold censure thou prayest ;
　That heart-sob in sleep is the mightiest prayer !
I have heard the proud pharisee follow the litany—
　Listened when thousands were chanting in praise ;
But that lute-soul that lay in the deep starry midnight
　Beside his " poor Edgar," has drowned with his lays
All the mocking and cantings of empty profession,
　And taught me to cover the wounds of my race,
And anoint them with spikenard, however so costly,
　And follow the erring through every disgrace !
Yea, follow ; till midnight shall break into morning,
　Till a heart-sob shall melt the misanthrope's chain,
And unbar all the doors, with its love and its warning,
　Which ever have held the poor sufferer in pain !

THE YOUNG MARTYR.

[NOTE.—The public can not have forgotten the intense excitement which
prevailed a few brief years since, in consequence of the cruel and merciless act
of that poor, deluded bigot, Rev. Mr. Lindsley, who whipped his little son to
death, because the child would not say his prayers, in obedience to the com
pulsory command of his infatuated father. The following poem is intended to
preserve as a future warning, this sorrowful drama in the history of modern
Orthodoxy.]

A strain of music caught my ear,
A strain devoid of mortal fear,
A strain that 'rose in warblings clear,
    Upon the summer air.

A vine-clad bower met my eye—
Birds flitted in that summer sky,
Or soared aloft on pinions high,
    And Nature seemed all fair.

Beyond, the gray old mountains stood
All reverent in silent mood,
And just anear, the grand old wood
    Bore royally its crown.

The busy hum of countless forms
Sipping from Nature's honeyed charms,
So free from tortures and alarms,
    Made glad my soul.

But o'er that sweet melodious strain
Which swept 'round Nature's sacred plain,
A sure emollient for all pain,
    One voice uprose.

A golden-haired, a meek-eyed child
Roamed out in Nature's sunny wild,
And then awoke that joyous wild
    With music all his own !

3

Birds chattered as they heard their song
Repeated by that mimic tongue,
And hid the rich green leaves among,
    To watch the mocking elf.

Winds raised with fingers all unseen
The golden locks which veiled that brain,
Then tenderly let fall again
    Those tresses rare.

All Nature seemed to be at peace,
And that young soul, so full of peace,
Did marvelous her power increase,
    On that fair day.

He bent above the clover-cups,
And perfumed bells where insect sups,
And caught the rainbow in the drops
    Of beaded dew.

He turned the hard and rounded stone
To find the ant at buried throne,
And hummed the beetle's monotone,
    While stooping there.

Then up he sprang and sought the sky—
The purple clouds went wheeling by—
He saw the swallows swifter fly,
    And mocked their lays.

From the black cloud the thunder rolled—
Still jorous, he the warning told,
As from his soul the power uprolled,
    In childish bass.

He saw a weary pilgrim sink
Beside the swift stream's mossy brink,
And call aloud for cooling drink,
    While fainting there.

From grotto near he snatched a shell,
And plunged it in the running well,
Then at the old man's feet he fell!
    "Drink, Father, drink!"

"Come home with me and share my bread,
And you shall have my trundle-bed,
And rest you there this weary head,
    And I will watch!"

But now the noonday hours had sped,
The thunder-cloud was overhead,
And suddenly I heard a tread,
    And loudest call.

Out from a shaded, latticed porch,
Peered a sharp face in earnest search,
And birds looked down from loftiest perch,
    With curious eye.

Then harshly rang that parent's voice,
And prated of his priestly choice,
Declaring liberty a vice,
    And crime most damnable!

"Come, say your prayers, my wicked son—
Say the commandments, one by one;
Now for these truant hours atone!"
    Speechless the child!

"Speak, child, 'tis time to go to bed;
Speak, or God's judgment overhead
May number you among the dead,
    This very night!

Repeat with me, and say you've sinned;
Confess to God that you have sinned,
Or you shall go with those who've sinned
    To deepest hell!

Speak now, I say, before I strike—
Before the hand of God doth strike!
Thou stubborn thing, so devil-like!"
    "I *can not*, father, dear!

Father, I've prayed with birds and flowers,
I've prayed in Nature's temple-bowers—
I've prayed with all that bless the hours,
    But can not pray the creed!

I do not love those cruel prayers
That cursed my first, my rosy years !
I have repeated all my prayers
          To God this day."

"Blasphemer, devil, heretic ! "
Then came a shower of blows so thick,
With demon cursings, that the click
          Of moments could not part them !

Fainting, the youthful martyr fell,
As dire command and hideous yell,
The breath of superstition's hell,
          Smote him in death !

O bigotry ! this is thy work,
And thou hast plunged thy bloody dirk
To heart of Christian, heart of Turk,
          By right canonical !

Thou hast provoked the people's ire ;
The world of judgment is on fire,
And Reason's truth shall never tire :
          Prepare, prepare !

IF thou wouldst be happy, preserve a clear conscience, and a healthy body, as a pure and fitting abode for the soul. Keep thy own sanctuary inviting, and it may prove to thee a paradise of peace, when war rages without. He who seeks happiness outside of his own resources must be doomed to disappointment; but he who appropriates that which lies within, is always supplied.

To cultivate a conscience void of offense toward all men, let us weigh our own faults against our neighbors' virtues, instead of weighing our own virtues against our neighbors' faults.   M. J. W.

IN THE CRUCIBLE.

[Note.—The following poem is based upon facts. A lady of fine native talent and many prepossessing qualities, formed an uncontrollable attachment for a clairvoyant physician of eminent skill and celebrity. This attachment on her part took on the character, ere long, of the most intensified love, and so enthusiastic was she in his praise, using all her efforts to secure patients for him, that no common observer could fail to detect her expectations for the future. In the midst of this prospective bliss a difference arose between the parties; and, chagrined and disappointed above measure, the lady soon formed a matrimonial alliance with another man.

From the hour of the quarrel above mentioned, this woman and her married accomplice lost no opportunity to vilify, malign, hunt and persecute her formerly idolized friend, the doctor. With the most persistent effort, she sought to destroy his practice, his reputation, and his very life, by the most artful and infamous falsehood that ever fouled a woman's lips. In time, the physician married the daughter of this woman's sister, a loving, gentle and devoted creature, whose friendship for the doctor was doubtless quickened into love by the most cruel and unreasonable retaliation of her aunt. And now, true to the spirit of vindictive hate, which had, viper-like, poisoned the very currents of her life, this woman continued her persecution, if possible, with more relentless fury than before, regardless of the feelings of his young and beautiful wife, whom she also distressed and persecuted by her most unfeeling conduct. At last, the young wife fell into hereditary consumption, and peacefully passed to the higher life, soon to be followed by her loved companion, who was then a confirmed invalid, and convalescing from an almost fatal sickness. Sweet words of forgiveness wreathed the lips of the crucified, as she pleasantly and calmly breathed her parting blessing upon her husband and mother, to whom she had left a legacy of love and devotion seldom equaled. It was at this juncture that disappointed love, now mad and drunken with indulgence, held its last high carnival! Regardless of every holy tie, insensible to every womanly instinct, this poor infatuated monomaniac incited her miserable tools to the work of desecration, and for nothing better than the paltry gratification of her diabolical revenge!

A *lawless farce* was enacted at the last resting-place of that peaceful form, and with the sombre pines of the grave-yard whispering rebuking sighs in the ears of the guilty resurrectionists, the holy silence was thus invaded by these pitiless conspirators, in the person of her husband and a medical attendant

whom he had duped! It is needless to say that the wicked plot failed most
signally, only in that it left a foul, an ineradicable stain upon the lives of these
most unfortunate criminals!

The poem purports to be spoken by the bereaved mother of the young and
faithful wife.]

Once I had a sister, beauteously fair,
Roses on her plump cheeks, sunbeams in her hair ;
Like a lamb she gamboled 'round me in her play,
How I loved that sister only God can say !
How I watched her motions, planned for future time,
Thought when I was older, how I'd set to rhyme
All her childish graces, all her blooming love,
Mingled with the vexing of my little dove !

When she laughed and frolicked rills went laughing too,
Hills and mountains rolicked in their vernal hue ;
When she fell to grieving, tear-drops clothed in night
All my world of beauty, once so grand and bright ;
When in sweetest singing all her tones were strung,
How their rising echoes heaven's music sprung ;
And I drank in power from that melting voice,
For I knew that angels did with me rejoice.

Yes ! one cradle rocked us, and one pair of arms
Lovingly wound 'round us, shielding from alarms ;
One gray roof above us, locked in sweet embrace,
Slept we on one pillow, nestling face to face.
The blushing rose and lily were never half so fair
As my beauteous sister, sunbeams in her hair,
Never woodland songster soothed me with such spell,
As the childish warblings that from her ripe lips fell !

Years rolled on all swiftly, duties led apart ;
Could I think a cobra was hatching in that heart !
Know a deadly serpent could slide into my bower—
Steal into our cradle—crush with such a power ?
Seed of direst envy sprouted in her way,
And I could not check it, or its trespass stay !
Heartless were its growers, tending it with care,
Parasite so deadly, blasting love so fair !

So it kept on creeping, coiling 'round that life,
With its tendrils weaving mean excuse for strife.

I tried to think that reason had tottered on its throne,
Tried to think repentance would in time atone—
Years rolled on ; I, lonely, trod my destined path,
Sealed my lips in silence, stayed unworthy wrath ;
Angels came and cheered me, wiped my tears away,
Pointed to the Faithful guarding all my day ;
Bade me seek a city, refuge of the soul,
Where the bells of welcome sweetest chimings toll,
So I sought to follow, burdened mortal I,
Drank in words of promise from dwellers in the sky !

Ere this, tender blossoms, quite as fresh and fair
As my early sister sunbeams in her hair,
Had lain upon my bosom, drawn their life from mine,
Made me feel how truly all children are divine.
I saw them swift maturing, and rich, concordant notes,
Like angel music lingering, like song that 'round us floats,
Had made me feel the virtue and worth of life below—
This happened ere my sister did envious from me go.

But of the cause be silent ; O pen of mine forbear !
And help me, blessed angels, as silently to bear !
It is enough to know it—how, held by envy's chain,
A child of God, immortal, can forge such dirk of pain !
For shall I e'er forget it, the stab I then received,
When they said, "A sister did it," and I so late bereaved ?
Three days of mortal anguish, such as no pen can write,
When reason quivered, faltered, and I swung from depth to height !

I gazed upon the heavens, holding my broken heart,
With the pointed dagger in it—that sharp and fiery dart !
Moments to ages swelling, crowded the bursting rain,
Closer, and closer, and closer—and prayer was all in vain.
Like mariner benighted, I looked for one ray of morn ;
One sign of love in that yawning crime—it grinned like a fiend in
    scorn :
And like a wild commingling, all sounds below, above,
Seemed whirling on in chaos, and the dagger deeper drove !

The mountains reeled and staggered as if they felt my grief,
The ocean gathered up its waves and hid each fatal reef !
My outer senses failed me in that hour of agony,
When Nature seemed to lift her voice and shout my spirit free !

While groans from out her great heart shook the web of things away,
And instincts stirring in my soul, her tongue did best portray !
Above, she spread her glory, as if to lull and charm
My storm-tossed being back to peace, my dying trust make warm.

All here seemed dread confusion, except one lonely spot,
Where Envy stood o'er my Beautiful, with shining blade so hot ;
The precious clay, so passive ; but grief in her streaming eyes,
Close stood the loosened spirit, and pointed to the skies !
Th re, countless souls were bending, wonder in their gaze,
Pity in their holy hearts, sorrow in their ways—
The dread, dread woe went over, the black cloud drifted along,
And my Beautiful Child stood foremost, one of that martyr-throng.
She pointed me "higher, higher," to the courts of the Faithful and
        True ;
Another went " *Guilty* " from me, on the cloud of leaden hue !

A calm from the court celestial swept down upon my soul,
A calm from the golden glory in soft waves touched my soul !
I sank in that sick slumber with the angels all around,
Soothing with costly ointment, the deep, the ghastly wound !
How long my spirit tarried in sweet, unconscious bliss,
I may never know in that world, can never know in this ;
But when I woke to mem'ry, this Old world was the New,
And lives were all laid open—I read them, *false* or *true!*
The wheel with its cruel grinding, the steel with its poison dart,
Had opened the soul's strong portals, unveiled each curtained heart.
I saw the art of piercing in all its deadly guise,
Like serpent in the cradle, coils near to fairest skies ;
And I rose from that Gehenna, with a purpose true and strong,
To strangle the viper, Envy ; and crush the demon, Wrong !

Now may the solemn dirges clothing this wounded heart,
Roll on in notes of warning, where'er the tear-drops start,
And raise to firm rebuking, a world so long oppressed,
Till the tongue shall feel its taming, and the hunted soul have rest !
The stars will set in darkness, though dazzling be their rays,
And Genius stoop, unworthy, though sweetest be its lays ;
The fairest hand strike keenest, the softest tongue destroy,
And seldom is the metal without ts base alloy !
But the HATE of thwarted woman can coin a life-long lie,
To gash her bleeding victims, nor stop it when they die !
The more she's foiled in purpose, more frenzied grows her art ;
A *stone* she treads on lightly, but stamps upon a HEART !

I mean no wrong to woman—she is my dearest friend,
But tell me how an angel can stoop to be a fiend !
Oh ! tell me how the lovely fall from such high estate,
To hunt, and tear, and torture, with sting of scorpion hate !

THE MAGDALEN.

[Given under the inspiration of Edgar A. Poe.]

In the Monumental City,
Where the angel hearts take pity
On God's feeble lambs there slaughtered,
On His homeless lambs there quartered ;
Where the races meet in sadness,
And the mob once drank, in madness,
Patriot blood—
In that place of fanes and towers,
Cenotaphs and sacred bowers,
Noble virtues, burning hate, matins early, orgies late.
Wealth and fashion, truth and passion,
Once I stood.

It was night ; the lamps were gleaming,
And the struggling stars were beaming
Through a cloud.
Grave and gay were rushing past me,
When a something ostled, pushed me,
Groaned aloud ;
And a slender, fragile being
Stood before me—checked her fleeing.
O, that sweet impassioned face,
O, that look of angel grace !
But so wan, so wild, so tearful !
At her glances something fearful

Threw its shadow 'cross my path ;
And I clasped the hapless being,
Plainly by the lamplight seeing
   " *Outcast* " on her marble brow !
   White her robes as driven snow,
She was rushing toward the river,
Where the lamplight shadows quiver—
   This her path !

" Oh, for God's sake, human brother,
Tell me, have you known a mother—
Have you known one as no other ? "
   Thought I of my loved Lenore !
Soothed I then her wild emotion,
Beating like the troubled ocean,
'Neath the storm-cloud all commotion,
   Beating, beating on the shore.
Spoke I kindly, for my reason
Oft betrayed by human treason,
Sore betrayed by mortal treason,
   'Rose above the passion-bowl.
In that lone and hapless being,
Unto death and darkness fleeing,
In her desperation fleeing,
   I beheld a woman-soul !

Then the claspings of my mother,
My true-hearted, angel mother,
And the pleadings of another
   I had loved, as none can tell !
Cradle hymns and morning kissings,
Drove away the serpent hissings,
Hushed the demon cobra hissings,
      Of my later hell !
Bowed I then as to an angel,
Stood before my soul's evangel,
For a woman was the angel
   Who had ever faithful been,
When the tempter lured me onward,
When the furies dragged me downward,
When the harpies hurled me downward,
   Into whirling depths of sin !

Yes, I bowed before *the woman!*
Promised God to be a true man—
　　Took her trembling hand in mine,
While she shook with childish sobbings,
And the sympathetic throbbings
　　Of my pitying for this vine,
With its vernal foliage fading,
With its finest tendrils wading
　　· Into crime,
Made it seem an hour of judgment,
When the gods all meet in judgment,
When the stones cry out in judgment,
　　On a nation's crime!

Then did inspiration fire me ;
Life with honors could not hire me ;
Oman's treasures could not buy me ;
Satan with his gifts might try me ;
With his flashing gems invite me ;
Send his hounds of hate to bite me ;
Scandal's crew to steal my name :
Soil my garments with his shame!
　　　　I was deaf ;
　　Deaf to all but love and truth !
　　Deaf to all but woman's truth !

I could only hear *the woman,*
While her life-notes, superhuman,
　　Mingled with professioned pity
　　In that monumental city,
Where the human tide kept beating,
Now advancing, now retreating—
　　Beating, beating, beating, beating,
Every phase of madness meeting
　　On that passion-haunted shore.
With the Magdalen before me,
Other angels hovered o'er me ;
One who in sore travail bore me,
Never ceased her vigils o'er me,
　　And my sainted, sweet Lenore!

Then I swore before the altar,
God's high throne and holy altar,

With a faith which can not falter,
I would break this chain and halter,
   Which makes man a slave ,
Steals his reason, drowns his pity,
Sends him reeling through the city,
   To a drunkard's grave ;
Freezes all his finer feelings,
Checks the sacred springs of healing;
   With a subtle calculation
   Of the cost of each libation,
Counts the paltry silver pieces
Which from woman's hand it fleeces,
   Robbing her of home and virtue,
   Giving lust for angel virtue,
Leaving blight, disease and shame,
With the brand of harlot name !

Though the bitter tide rolled o'er me,
And to drunkard's grave they bore me,
Now the voice of gentle woman,
Now the form of pitying woman,
   Are the means by which I speak :
And I pray you, human brother,
By the sacred name of "*brother*,"
By the holy name of "*mother* "
By your soul-love and no other,
Help me rend this chain and halter—
Let us never, never falter,
   Till its power we break !

THE SIBYL'S WARNING.

[The reading public are well in'ormed of the present movement of the Or-
tbodox church in this country, by which it demands the mutilation of our Constitution and the utter destruction of our " inalienable right " to the exercise
of private thought and judgment, independent of all ecclesiastical authority.

This " right " has proven the key-note of our Republican system, the axis upon which its whole machinery swings, as forever defying and preventing the sub-ordination of the secular to any sectarian power. That the High CHURCH of America, both Catholic and Protestant, has been biding its time, determined to undermine and subvert the principles of our immortal charter, viz, *Freedom of the religious thought, and Universal Toleration*, no one can longer deny. At last, " the logic of events " has proven it.

A scheme which Catholicism had scarcely dared to whisper outside of its synods one hundred years ago, it has now unblushingly blurted in the faces of free-born Americans for the last ten years, and wi h the most astonishing self-conceit and impudence, considering that it owed its foothold, its wealth and influence here upon republican soil, to the very system of toleration it now so loudly condemns! But strong in its increase of wealth and concentration of numbers, it has boldly and truthfully declared itself; and as an illustration, we refer you to an important work by J. S. Van Dyke, A. M., " Popery, the Foe of the Church and the Republic," a copy of which should be in every household of our land, as a true compilation and digest of Catholicism in Amer-ica. Free schools, a free press, and a free consci nce, are here shown to be among the most execrable of all things to the Papacy—"that fatal license of which we can not entertain too much horror."—[Pope Pius.] " I would rather a half of the people of this nation should be brought to the stake and burned, than one man should read the Bible and form his judgments from its con-tents."—[From " The Freeman's Journal " in Popery, page 267.] How then, in the case of other literature, radically liberal?

" Liberty of conscience is an absurd and dangerous maxim." " Laymen have nothing to do but to hear and submit."—["Popery," page 268.] "Protestants are not to inquire whether the Catholic church is hostile to civil and religious lib-erty, or not." " If the Papacy be founded in divine right, it is supreme over whatever is founded only in human right, and then *your institutions should be made to harmonize with it, and not it with your institutions* " "*Liberty of conscience is unknown to the Catholics. The word 'Liberty' should be banished from the domain of religion.* It is neither more nor less than a fiction to say that a man has the right to choose his own religion "—[" Popery," page 249.] " The rebellion of priests is not treason, for they are not subject to civil gov-ernment."—[*Ibid*, page 246.] " It is the duty of the Roman Catholic church to compel heretics, by corporeal punishment, to submit to her faith "—[Dens' Theology, a Catholic text-book.] " Heretics, who are forgers of the faith, are justly punished with death."—[St. Thomas, in " Popery."] " Let the public school system go to where it came from—the devil."—[Freeman's Journal, Dec. 11, 1869.] " This country has no other hope, politically or mor lly, ex-cept in the vast and controlling extension of the Catholic religion."—[Free-man's Journal.] " It will be a glorious day for the Catholics in this coun ry, when under the blows of justice and morality our school system will be shiv-ered to pieces. Until then, modern Paganism will triumph."—[Catho.ic Tel.

In view of the undeniable assumptions of the Papacy in these United S ates, it is the more surprising, that by means of a Protestant Union, the Orthodox church of America should seek to accomplish just what the Romish church most of all desires, as the first step toward the union of the spiritual and civil powers in this country. Though Catholicism is known to be the deadly foe of Protestantism, the American church (Orthodox), in its rash zeal to arrest the spread of Heterodoxy or Rationalism, has planted itself at last before the high court of this nation, demanding the surrender of all that is truly republican, by the insertion of clauses intended to compel subserviency to its own creed, and rob all honest dissenters of their equal rights before the law. We quote from the words of F. E. Abbot, editor of *The Index*, Toledo, Ohio, Feb. 10th, 1872: "If the proposed changes are ever made in the Constitution, their necessary result will be to prevent all persons, except Christian believers, from holding any office, civil or military, under the American Government. No honest believer in the newly incorporated doctrines will be able to take the oath of allegiance required from all United States officials and soldiers. Only Christian believers and dishonest disbelievers will be able to take it; consequently the entire power of the government, both political and military, will be constitutionally concentrated in the hands of those who believe, or profess to believe, the doctrines thus incorporated. Whether intended now or not, oppressive persecution must be the consequence of the adoption of the proposed amendment. Persecution will grow like a cancer in the body politic just as soon as the coveted inequality of religious rights once poisons its blood. The movement in which those men are engaged* has too many elements of strength to be contemned by any far-seeing liberal. Blindness or sluggishness to-day means SLAVERY to-morrow. Radicalism must pass now from thought to action, or it will deserve the oppression that lies in wait to overwhelm it."

Utterly blind seemingly, to the formidable growth and power of the Roman Catholic church in this country, these Protestant descendants of the Puritans, who fled from religious intolerance and oppression in the Old World are now first to initiate that same hierarchy of Church and State from which they fled only about two hundred and fifty years ago; and the "*heresy*" of free thought has become almost as hateful to them as to the bloody Montford of ancient inquisitorial celebrity! Couched in the artful drapery of soft words and pious entreaty, as is the memorial of this party, signed by leading bishops, judges and ex-officers all over our land, we can not but plainly discover the jeweled blade which may at one fell blow strike at the heart of American Liberty, and usher in the most fearful war of modern history. And while in all conventions and synods of the recent Protestant "Church union," great stress is laid upon "the dangerous increase of infidelity"—"the necessity of combining, in order to become a power for the suppression of Rationalism, Spiritualism," etc., how can these foolhardy violators of our royal charter fail to see what the bitter end must be, and that they are not less heretical to the Roman Catholic church, than the Rationalists of this country are to them? Then, when they declare "the time has come to put down this her sy'" of free thought, this infidelity in our land, let them not forget there is another Lion in the way, which may walk into the fold they so ruthlessly throw wide open and consign them also to the altar of sacrifice! In earnest entreaty and faithful obedience to the spirit of prophecy, we present to all who dare betray the sacred cause of Human Liberty, *the Sibyl's warning.*

* The National Convention, to secure the religious amendment of the United States Constitution, held in Thoms' Hall, Cincinnati, Wednesday, Jan. 31st, and Thursday, Feb. 1st, 1872.]

Come on ! we're ready for the fray,
And know who wins in freedom's day.
The flames of Salem light again
Upon Columbia's battle-plain !

We've made the British lion roar
In echoes kissing all our shore ;
Americans can drown the tea
Which costs too much for liberty !

Come on ! with Mather in the van,
The fires of Smithfield 'round us fan ;
We live to die, and die to live,
That higher freedom we may give.

Import some inquisition grand,
And gag the THINKERS of our land !
Ha ! do you know that millions bold,
Will seige the tyrant in his hold ?

Come on ! we give you oil and wine,
The vintage pure of Freedom's vine,
Whene'er ye give us freedom too;
But this deny, the cost ye'll rue !

We've done with priestly art and lies—
We spurn its cunning and disguise !
Our right to speak we will defend,
And heaven will fresh power send !

Come on ! the martyred souls above
Are standing by us with their love ;
And now we face the tyrant CREED,
And bid the living gospel speed !

We'll bear it with a stronger hand,
Since Judas with his Roman band,
Has sought to crucify our Lord,
And now denied the living word !

Come on ! my people long distressed,
By robbers stealing from your nest ;

THE VESTAL.

Remember all those long crusades,
Which cursed the earth with "holy" raids!

Remember all the yokes and chains
Which made men cattle on the plains,
And beasts of burden, everywhere!
Did they "the loaves and fishes" share?

No, no! the crumb and hardened crust,
And often into prison thrust!
The starving family at home—
The fairest in the early tomb!

The last cow taken for the rent—
The homeless to the mountain sent,
To find rest in its friendly caves,
Which Popes transformed to crowded graves!

Great God! shall I, a mortal, cease
To raise my voice at this increase
Of Bigotry upon the soil
So crimsoned by the blood of toil?

So lately washed to free the slave,
By blood of fathers, brothers brave!
And now the gem that tempts a foe
Who always gave the deadliest blow?

Shall Freedom be to us a name,
And history write our nation's shame?
Shall foes blot out our sacred stars,
And usher in the olden wars?

The answer comes from hill and dale,
From ocean, where our navies sail;
It comes from whirring wheel and band,
And countless looms throughout our land!

It comes from ringing scythe and blade,
Whose voices echo through the glade;
It comes from massive ribs of steel,
Which bind our old ship's heavy keel!

Our Ship of State, equipped and manned
By free-born THINKERS of this land,
Will yet outride the storm of CRAFT,
Which goes to war in open raft!

From Lexington and Bunker Hill
Grand memories will our spirits thrill,
And stalwart forms in magic rise
From every land beneath the skies!

Ho! proud invader, ours the blood
Sent down from where the Fathers stood—
Our heroes, Jefferson and Paine,
And Washington, of royal name!

And them ye owe for all this might,
Ye have enjoyed by *common right*—
But touch our charter, that despise,
Ye tempt the watch of countless eyes!

Connive, with oily words and bland,
Insist you would "protect" the land;
Talk of "the great increase of sin,"
And urge it, till your aim ye win!

Your Sumpter sound across the sea—
Awake the armies of the free;
Ha! have ye seen from whence they come,
When heaven decrees your final doom?

Up from the dungeon and the fire—
The millions ye have robbed of hire!
Out from the furnace and the mills—
Out from the rocks, and woods, and hills!

The blood which flows in freemen's veins
Is ripening like the fruits and grains;
Our common schools, our common laws,
Have bound us in one Common Cause!

Touch but the meanest son of all,
Because he THINKS, and you shall fall!

Millions of souls will swear your doom,
And find for its fulfillment room!

So do not rashly tempt the Fates,
And rouse these just and fiery hates!
We give you warning—heed it not,
The conflict will be fierce and hot!

Nor will it cease, till all your chains,
Are banished from Columbia's plains,
And you are shorn of priestly pride,
And will our·royal oath abide!

This oath to free, and not enslave—
Make self-reliant, truly brave;
Rescue the mind from creedish thrall,
And make wise THINKERS of us all!

LOVE AND LUST—THE DIFFERENCE.

Love is lasting, lust is shifting,
    All unrest and ever drifting;
Love adores and saves its object,
    Lust would make all virtue subject.
Love subordinates low feeling,
    Lust lives on by double-dealing;
Love doth bear the heaviest crosses,
    Lust ne'er counts its victim's losses;
Love doth bridle speech and action,
    Lust for law hath no attraction;
Love doth pity, breathe compassion,
    Lust doth spurn such kindly fashion;
Love doth lavish all protection,
    Lust doth urge to misdirection.

Love disease and woe would banish,
    Lust would make all beauty vanish ;
Love in use and joy abideth,
    Lust in base indulgence hideth ;
Love doth give the hearty hand-clasp,
    Lust may give, but with the death-grasp ;
Love builds homes and makes them brighter,
    Lust its withering chain draws tighter.
Love is an angel, Lust is a devil,
    Stalking where furious passions revel ;
Love is the voice that cheers the dying,
    Lust is the coward his victim flying ;
Love is the sunlight, warm and cheering,
    Lust is the dread flame we go fearing ;
Love is the hope that cheers the living,
    Lust is the lease that dies with the giving.
Love is savior and redeemer,
    Lust a fraud—a treacherous schemer !
Love doth selfishness despise,
    Lust never bloated self denies.
Love spikenard pours on broken hearts,
    Lust seeks fresh victims for his arts ;
"Love is fulfilling of the law,"
    Lust is a traitor—scorns that saw !
Love gives worth, and wealth, and labor,
    Lust robs dearest friend and neighbor ;
Love is the coin that always blesses,
    Lust is the counterfeit that curses ;
Love is of home the light and charmer,
    Lust the destroyer, deadly harmer ;
Love wins sweetly, all devotion,
    Lust makes a hell—a wild commotion !
Love yields fruits of the richest flavor,
    Lust wrecked hopes and a rotten savor ;
Love is the tried and true availer,
    Lust is the lawless vile assailer ;
Love doth bloom in happy faces,
    Lust doth lurk in low disgraces ;
Love may promise, none to doubt him,
    Lust may swear good faith—we scout him !
Love is the freedom time makes stronger,
    Lust is the slavery time makes longer ;
Love doth lead to the noblest teachers,

THE VESTAL.

Lust doth abhor all faithful preachers ;
Love doth brave the greatest danger,
    Lust is to courage true a stranger ;
Love doth unmask the frowning despot,
    Lust in excuse is a senseless bigot ;
Love doth exalt both man and woman,
    Lust is the foe of all that is human !

"AS SHEEP WITHOUT A SHEPHERD."

Coasting by the solemn seas,
Some in prayer upon their knees,
Screened among the wild-wood trees,
Where the lions on them seize,
    Find we God's own lambs !

Climbing mountains wild and high,
Gazing deeply in the sky,
Sinking lone, with groan and sigh,
As they sheared and naked lie,
    We behold these lambs !

Pressing through the tangled dell,
Where the wolves in hunger yell,
Hunted to the gates of hell,
Where the oft despairing fell,
    See these panting lambs !

Driven through the crowded street,
With their torn and bleeding feet,
Little pity do they meet,
From the priestly mercy-seat—
    Homeless, captive lambs !

Tyrants forge the heavy chain,
Build their towers on fairest plain,
Harvests hold of golden grain,
Grown of service, grown in pain,
   By these burdened lambs !

Temples rise of royal mould,
Burnished bright with stolen gold,
Price of millions meanly sold,
Choicest of the heavenly fold—
   Choicest of our lambs !

Priestly court and equipage,
Bought by death of saint and sage,
Blotting life's historic page,
Crushing with its fiery rage,
   Offers up these lambs !

Never once has priestcraft failed
To claim the offering it has nailed
To the cross, where it has railed
At its victim there impaled—
   Passive, bleeding lamb !

Never has it victim saved,
But upon the ages graved,
Picture of the power it craved,
Stained with blood in which it laved
   All our dying lambs !

Borne across the solemn seas,
Wafted by the changeful breeze,
Hear we now angelic pleas,
Lifting nations from their knees—
   All these fettered lambs !

Now, throughout the spacious sky,
Justice lets her arrows fly—
Judgment calls from throne on high,
To each nation far or nigh,
   " Peter *feed* my lambs ! "

Lo ! the day drives back the night,
Men are rising in their might,
Gog and Magog meet in fight,
Angels raise the banner, RIGHT,
        O'er our wounded lambs !

Stars are brighter as they guide,
Planets swifter as they ride,
Oceans bolder in their tide,
Armies firmer, side by side,
        As they free our lambs !

Seraphs chant their sweetest lays,
Systems swell terrestrial praise,
O the grand, victorious lays,
Pouring full in sacred blaze,
        On our rescued lambs !

Weary, foot-sore, wounded, come !
O'er the desert press ye home,
In our Father's house find room !
Youth shall there in radiant bloom,
Rising from the mouldy tomb,
Read each tyrant's final doom—
        Saved our snow-white lambs !

WHAT is toleration in a true sense ? It is a kindly recognition of
another person's honest opinion, though it be radically opposed to our
own. Any malicious treatment of another, because simply differing
in opinion, betrays a narrow, selfish and contemptible spirit.

A due regard for the rights of others ensures confidence and esteem,
while the reverse of this spirit parts many friends.

THE DAUGHTER'S REQUEST TO A DYING FATHER.

Come to me, father, come in the early morning,
   And waken to a riper, richer duty ever ;
And should a danger threaten, give me warning,
   And arduous coilings of my adversaries sever.

Come to me, father, when fades out my nooning,
   And sinks my sun adown the evening sky :
I've passed the weary time, the trial—swooning,
   And now more joyfully my labor-moments fly !

Come to me, father, when the sun departing
   Flings back upon my silvered head its generous rays ;
And call me "Jennie," as in childhood's gay disporting,
   You gamboled with, and chased me through the olden ways.

Come to me, father, when the twilight folding,
   Wraps me in silence, in the holy hush of night,
And then, perchance my spirit-eye beholding,
   May gaze upon you with reality's delight !

Come to me, father, when the midnight shading
   Holds me in rapt communion with the world I seek ;
And as my mortal stars grow dim, misty, and fading,
   Meet me, aye, meet me at my new Morn's golden gate !

BEWARE of the slanderer. Beware of the insinuator the mischief maker, the envious and revengeful. Beware of him who would give you friendship only by the sacrifice of your individuality and your principles. It is a dangerous experiment to purchase favor of one by consenting to a wrong against another.

"HE HAS GONE."

He has gone to the land where eternity's bloom
Shall burst on his vison o'er sorrow and gloom.
With the wealth of his blessing I battle the waves,
Nor fear I the conflict, or City of Graves !

For soon I will follow—he rush to embrace
And welcome me there in that city of peace.
O blessed re-union awaiting the true,
When this warfare is ended—this journey is through !

I look on this world wrapped in darkness and storm,
To feel *there* is sunshine, abounding and warm ;
I look on its trials, affliction and death,
As fading and transient—a bubble and breath.

But out of this fading, and out of this change,
What wonders surprise me, what mysteries strange !
The soul moves triumphant above the prone clay,
And joyfully enters its Temple of Day !

Dear father, thy blessing I hold to my heart ;
It shall comfort and soothe me when scorn sends his dart ;
It shall make me defiant when bigots arise,
And seek to ensnare me, or veil my bright skies !

Dear father, I listen, I wait for thy voice ;
Thou art gone from thy suffering—my soul doth rejoice !
And when we shall meet in that mansion above,
We shall know how unbroken the bright chain of Love !

FINIS.